Once, a pig built up a house.
The house was of straw that he bought from the town.

One day, a wolf came and saw the little pig.
He came to the pig's door, and then the wolf said . . .

TRAP 3 Little Pigs

By: Kyle Exum

First paperback edition June 2019
ISBN: 9781076641489

Published by Kyle Exum
www.Trap3LittlePigs.com

So I huffed, and I puffed, and I blew that thing down.
Next thing I knew, he was running around . . .

So I chased that pig down.
Wanted some bacon, so I had to
go to his big brother's house.

Said I blew that thing down.
Little Red Riding Hood didn't
ride home, so I'm after you now.

I'm a real alpha wolf, this ain't Little Bo Peep.
Don't try and cry "wolf," I ain't here for no sheep.
No McDonald's money, so y'all are my treat
and if we do the race, all I need are some cleats.

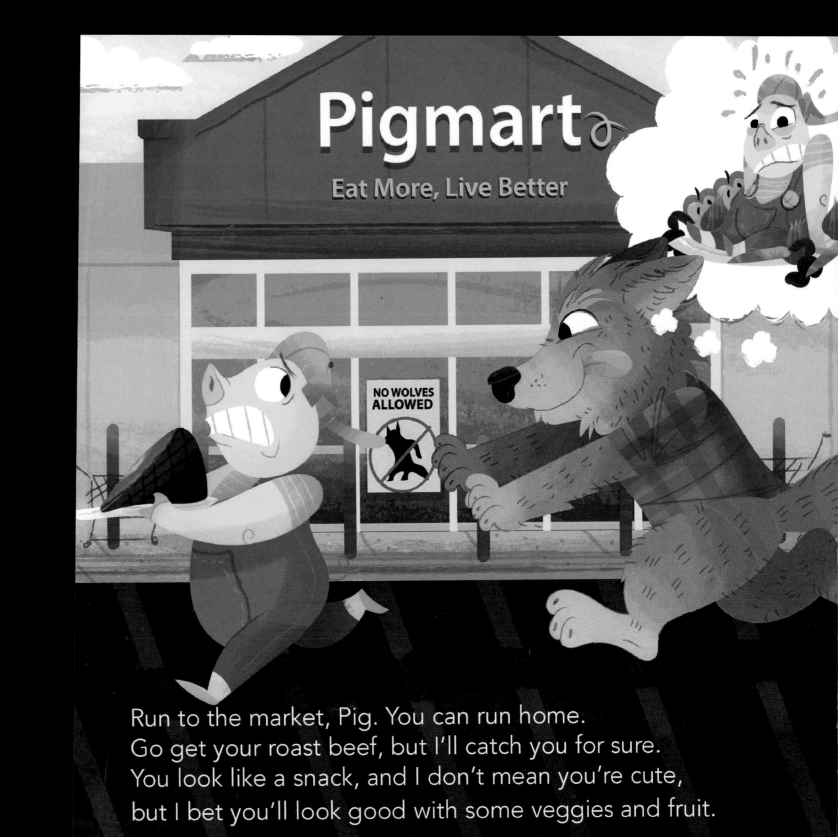

Run to the market, Pig. You can run home.
Go get your roast beef, but I'll catch you for sure.
You look like a snack, and I don't mean you're cute,
but I bet you'll look good with some veggies and fruit.

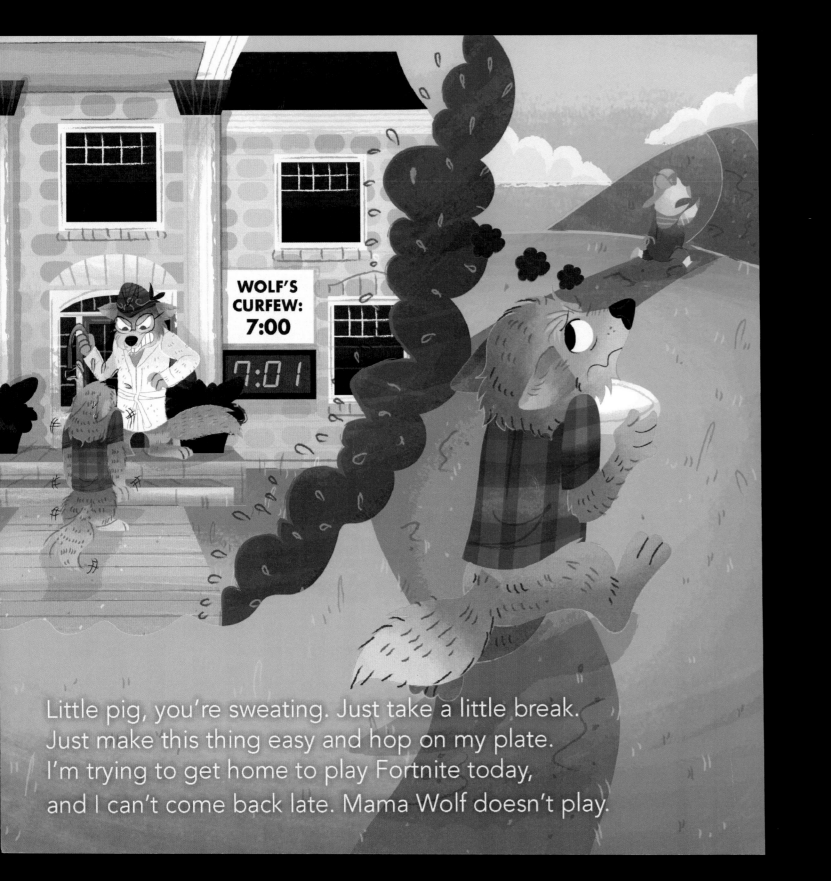

Little pig, you're sweating. Just take a little break.
Just make this thing easy and hop on my plate.
I'm trying to get home to play Fortnite today,
and I can't come back late. Mama Wolf doesn't play.

Pig told the wolf, "Oh, I'm leaving.
Mama ain't make me this thick to be eaten.
You're big and bad till my big bro gets even,
and no, I won't slow. Wolf, I trained for track season."

Don't run up that hill, Pig. You're not Jack and Jill.
Don't climb up that wall, have a great fall for real.
I need food to serve while I go on this date,
so don't make me look bad. I can't make Wolfy wait.

Lucky for Pig, I had worn the wrong kicks,
so he got to his brother's house made out of sticks.
Wolf came up after and saw the little pigs.
He came to the pigs' door, and then the wolf said . . .

So I huffed, and I puffed, and I blew that thing down.
Next thing I knew, they were running around . . .

So I chased those pigs down.
Wanted some bacon, so I had to
go to their big brother's house.

Said I blew that thing down.
Little Red Riding Hood didn't
ride home, so I'm after you now.

I'm a real alpha wolf, this ain't Winnie the Pooh.
Don't try to cry "wolf," I'm not lying to you.
My McDonald's money is low, so you'll do.
And I've got the right shoes, so it's over for you!

Come here little pigs, I need my two-course meal.
This is a fairy tale, but I'm for real.
I had Mary's little lamb, but a wolf's hungry still.
I need food that will fill.

I need some bacon! I need some fries!
I need some pork with some pie on the side!
I need some sausage with beans and some rice!
I need that candlelit dinner tonight!

Pig told the wolf, "Oh, you're tripping for real. I'm way too cute for a snack; I'm a meal. We came from the mud. We've had worse wolves we've beat. Yes, we're the pigs, but you don't want this beef!"

You know what, little pig, I'm tired. I'm not here to play.
If I don't bring dinner, I won't have a bae.
You don't even follow me back on the gram,
so don't think you can beat me. I'm about to go ham!

Lucky for them, I had tripped on a stick,
so they made it to their brother's house made of brick.
Wolf came up after and saw the little pigs.
He came to the pigs' door, and then the wolf said . . .

So I huffed, and I puffed, trying to blow that thing down,
but the house was of brick, and it stayed in the ground.

So I blew even harder, a real wolf won't quit.
No, I'm not chief, but I swear this is it!

And I would have had that pig's house blown into bits, but my asthma was acting up. I had to sit.

One pig said, "He stopped blowing his hot breath."
They heard footsteps and knew what was next.

So they played their mixtape, got the fireplace lit.
Then, they waited for Wolf to come in.

Pigs, I'm coming down the chimney,
about to fatten up like Santa Claus . . .

Made in the USA
Lexington, KY
25 July 2019